nickelodeon™

5-Minute Girl-Power Stories

Random House 🏠 New York

rhcbooks.com

ISBN 978-1-9848-9490-8

MANUFACTURED IN CHINA

10 9 8 7 6 5 4 3 2 1

CONTENTS

One warm, sunny day, Ryder and the pups were setting up their campsite. They had tents, sleeping bags, and plenty of ingredients for s'mores!

Skye noticed something in the sky. She called to her friends.

It was a plane! Ace was teaching Mayor Goodway how to fly. The mayor was nervous, but she was doing well, so Ace decided it was time for her to fly by herself. She released the controls.

"Take it away, Mayor Goodway. It's all you!" Ace said.

After a few bumps, it was smooth flying for the mayor . . . until a flock of birds flew by. They bumped into the plane wing, causing a piece to break loose!

Ace knew she had to fix the plane, and fast! She told a worried Mayor Goodway her plan to go out and fix the wing.

"Just keep flying straight, just keep flying straight," Mayor Goodway chanted to herself as Ace made her way along the edge of the wing.

When Ace reached down, her sleeve got caught on the broken wing! Luckily, she had a backup plan.

"Mayor Goodway, it's time to call the PAW Patrol!" she shouted over the wind.

With a little help from Chickaletta, Mayor Goodway called
Ryder and explained their problem.

"We'll be right there," Ryder told her. "No plane is too high,
no pup is too small!"

He called the PAW Patrol to the Air Patroller, and they took off.

Meanwhile, Ace's plane began shaking in the wind. The turbulence caused Chickaletta to bounce out of the plane and onto the other wing!

"Oh, no!" cried Mayor Goodway. But she couldn't help Chickaletta. She had to keep flying the plane.

Help soon arrived. Robo Dog flew the Air Patroller right above Ace's plane.

"Rocky, Skye—it's go time!" Ryder announced.

Skye and Rocky flew down to the plane.

Skye landed first, right behind the mayor.
"Yay! You did it, Mayor Goodway!" Skye cheered.
"Now *you* do it," said the mayor, relieved to have
an experienced pilot in charge again.
Skye took control of the plane and kept it steady.

Next it was Rocky's turn to help. He started by using his scissors to cut Ace's sleeve and free her from the wing.

"Thank you, Rocky!" Ace cried, hugging the hero pup.

"Way to go, Rocky. Now see if you can fix that wing!" said Ryder. Rocky got right to work.

Once she was free, Ace headed to the other wing to save Chickaletta.

"Operation Save Poor Little Chicky-Wicky in effect!" Ace shouted.

"I can't bear to look!" Mayor Goodway said.

Ace tried to grab Chickaletta, but a gust of wind blew the chicken right off the plane!

"We have an airborne chicken!" Ryder called to the pups.
"Marshall, I'm going to need you to catch her, and fast!"

"I'm all fired up," Marshall barked, running to the plane's exit.
He dove toward Chickaletta and made it to her just in time!
Chickaletta landed safely on Marshall's head.

As Marshall returned Chickaletta to the grateful Mayor Goodway, Rocky put the finishing touches on the wing. It was as good as new!

"Thanks, Skye," said Ace. "*Amazing* flying. I've got it from here." She returned to her seat in the cockpit.

Skye was excited that Ace had praised her flying! She and the rest of the pups headed back to the Air Patroller.

That night, the whole group gathered around a campfire to celebrate.

"Thanks, PAW Patrol. You really saved us! And my plane," Ace said to the pups over s'mores.

The PAW Patrol cheered, happy about another job well done.

It was spring-cleaning day at Sunny's salon! Blair loved to keep everything tidy, but Rox preferred things to be a little messy. The girls were discussing their plans when a new customer came in and sat in Sunny's salon chair.

"Hi, I'm Hannah," said the visitor. "I'm dancing in the new ballet!"

"We all love ballet!" Sunny told her. "What can we do for you?" she asked as the girls began gathering their tools.

Hannah needed a stay-put style for her performance that night. Sunny gave her a tight ballerina bun, adding super-sticky hair spray as the finishing touch.

"Not a hair out of place!" Hannah said. "Could you come and do the other ballerinas' hair before the show?"

Sunny agreed to help.

Hannah happily twirled out of the store.
"And don't forget that super-sticky hairspray," she called.
"We'll be there," Sunny replied. "Have a sunny day!"

"I'm all out of super-sticky hairspray," Sunny told her friends when they were alone again.

Blair saw a bottle on a high shelf. She grabbed a ladder and climbed up to get it.

"We don't need a ladder," Rox said. "I'm an expert jumper."

Rox jumped up and knocked the bottle down, and she and Blair reached out to grab it. But the bottle opened in the air and spilled on them both!

"We're stuck together!" said Blair.

After trying to pull away from each other and wash off the stickiness with shampoo, the girls were still stuck.

"Are you two *Blox* now?" Doodle joked about combining their names.

Sunny found the bottle and read the instructions aloud. "'In the event of unplanned sticking, create an unsticking solution with crab apples, sugar, water, and salt.'"

That was it! The three girls headed to the van to gather the ingredients.

Sunny drove them all to the orchard
to meet with Timmy.
"We have a code-red sticky situation,"
Sunny told him.

Timmy led the girls through the orchard to look for crab apples. They found a creek, and then a crab apple tree! They quickly grabbed the crab apples they needed and headed back to the Glam Van.

Next, they went to visit Cindy at her bakery. She was busy making a big order of pink cupcakes for the ballerinas.

"Whoa, what happened!" Cindy exclaimed when she saw Rox and Blair. Sunny explained the problem and asked for some sugar, which Cindy was more than happy to provide. The girls still needed water and salt. Luckily, Sunny knew where to find both.

The sea!

Sunny drove her friends to the beach. The girls jumped out of the van and ran toward the pier. But the water was far down from there. They needed something to scoop up the water!

"What about this gel tub?" Blair suggested.

"Great thinking!" said Sunny. She braided some ribbons together to make a rope and got out the super-sticky hair spray to make the tub and ribbons stick together. But as she was finishing her invention, the bottle spilled again. Sunny's hands were stuck to the railing!

Blair and Rox realized they could fix the mess if they worked together. They finished Sunny's invention, scooped up the salt water, and mixed it with the crab apples and sugar.

"Now, *that's* teamwork," Sunny said, praising her friends.

They poured some of the liquid on Sunny's hands . . . and it worked! She was unstuck!

"Woo-hoo!" the girls shouted after Sunny unstuck Blair and Rox. They were happy that they weren't stuck together anymore, but it also felt weird.

"I was getting used to being stuck to you," Blair said.

"Want me to stick you two back together?" Sunny joked to her friends. Laughing, the girls rushed to the ballet.

Sunny and her friends made it just in time to do the other ballerinas' hair.

"This is definitely one for the Style Files," Sunny said, taking a picture of the ballerinas.

Then they enjoyed the performance, which featured Doodle! It's a sunny day when friends stick together!

Dora's Farm Rescue!

Dora and Boots were exploring the farm one sunny afternoon when they heard a noise.

"Dora! Boots! Help, help! ¡Ayúdenme!" called Mami Pig. "My three little piggies are missing!"

"Don't worry," Dora replied. "We can find those little piggies!"

Dora and Boots called for Map.

"I know where you can find the three little piggies," said Map. "In the Big Red Barn! They're stuck! To get to the Big Red Barn, we have to go over the Duck Pond and through the Corn Maze."

"First, we need to find the Duck Pond," said Dora.

"I see a lot of ponds, but which one is the Duck Pond?" asked Boots.

"¡Mira! Look! There it is!" said Dora.
"Come on! ¡Vámonos!"

Dora, Boots, and Mami Pig arrived at the Duck Pond. They needed to cross a bridge. But when Boots tried to open the gate, he found it was locked!

"We've got to find a way to open this gate!" cried Mami Pig.
"It looks like the key to the gate was on this branch," said Dora.
"It must have fallen into one of these nests."

"I see it!" squealed Mami Pig. "The key is in the nest with four eggs."

Dora and Boots counted the eggs in each nest. "¡Uno, dos, tres, cuatro! Four eggs!"

Boots politely asked the mother duck for the key, then passed it to Dora. Dora unlocked the gate, and the three of them ran across the bridge.

Soon Dora, Boots, and Mami Pig got to a fork in the path.
"Which way leads to the Corn Maze?" asked Mami Pig.
The group searched for the footprints that matched Mami
Pig's, which they knew would lead them to the piggies.
"Over here!" shouted Boots, pointing to the right footprints.
"All right!" cheered Dora. "Let's follow them!"

They arrived at the Corn Maze.

"How do we get through it, Dora?" asked Boots.

A friendly scarecrow told them, "To get through my maze, you need to take the path that is amarillo."

"The yellow path!" Dora said. "Thank you, Mr. Scarecrow! ¡Gracias!"

Dora, Boots, and Mami Pig followed the yellow path out of the Corn Maze.

"We made it to the Big Red Barn!" cheered Dora.

Together they opened the door to the barn. It was very dark inside.

"I can't see anything," said Mami Pig nervously. "How will I find

"Let's see if Backpack has something that can help us see in the dark," Dora said.

Backpack gave them a flashlight. But before Dora could turn it on, they heard a noise. "That sounds like Swiper the Fox," said Dora.

"Oh, no!" said Boots. "That sneaky fox will try to swipe our flashlight!"

Dora, Boots, and Mami Pig shouted, "Swiper, no swiping! Swiper, no swiping!"

Swiper snapped his fingers. "Oh, mannn," he groaned
as he ran away.

After Swiper left, Dora shined the flashlight all around the barn.

"I see the piggies!" she said excitedly.

Mami Pig was so happy to see her babies!

"Gracias, Dora! Thanks, Boots!" said Mami Pig.
The three little piggies gave Dora and Boots some juicy red apples to thank them for helping.
"What a *farm*-tastic adventure!" said Dora, giggling. "We did it!"

SUPER GUPPIES!

Guppy Girl and her sidekick, Bubble Boy, were Super Guppies! Bubble Boy was super strong and could trap anything in a bubble, and Guppy Girl was super fast and shot water from her bracelet. Together, they used their powers to protect their home, Big Bubble City.

Sid Fishy was an evil villain.

Using smelly socks, garbage, and rotten eggs, he cooked up a disgusting concoction called stink sauce!

One night, the police had Sid Fishy cornered in his stink blimp.

"Stop right there, Sid Fishy. You're under arrest!" one officer said through her megaphone.

"I don't think so. Squirt them with the stink sauce!" Sid commanded his accomplice, who covered them in a stinky, slimy green goo.

"Smell you later, Officers," Fishy laughed as he made his escape.

It was clear that only Guppy Girl and Bubble Boy would be able to stop Sid from stinking up the city!

While the stink sauce was diabolical, Sid Fishy's master plan was far more sinister.

"I'm gonna fill this cloud up with stink sauce, and when it's full, it's gonna stink *all over* Big Bubble City!" Sid told his sidekick.

Bubble Boy and Guppy Girl saw the cloud begin
to fill up and jumped into action. They flew straight
toward the blimp and used their powers to fight Sid.

But Sid's stink sauce was too much for them.
They needed a new plan.

"We've got to stop him before he fills that cloud
with more stink," Guppy Girl said.

They decided to split up. Bubble Boy headed into the blimp to try to turn off the machine. But Sid Fishy caught him! He stuck Bubble Boy to the tank with his stink sauce.

"Looks like somebody's in a sticky situation," Sid said. "Almost full! Nothing can stop me now."

"Oh, yeah?" said a voice behind him.

Sid turned and saw Guppy Girl! He sprayed his stink sauce on her, but it didn't seem to have any effect.

"Huh? Guppy Girl, why aren't you moving?" Sid asked, creeping toward the still figure.

"Because that's not Guppy Girl!" Bubble Boy said triumphantly as the real Guppy Girl freed him from his stinky binding. Guppy Girl had used a cardboard cutout to distract Sid Fishy, and it worked!

Before Sid could act again, Bubble Boy trapped him in a super bubble. Guppy Girl put the pump in reverse and sucked all the stink out of the cloud.

"You're coming with us, Sid," Bubble Boy announced.

Later, at Big Bubble City Jail, Sid confessed that he had wanted to make everyone stinky because *he* was stinky and nobody wanted to be around him! He thought if he made everyone stinky, they'd be his friends.

Guppy Girl got a *great* idea.

"Let's get you cleaned up," she said.
Bubble Boy and Guppy Girl used their powers to give everyone a bubble bath!
Thanks to the Super Guppies, Big Bubble City was safer—and cleaner—than ever!

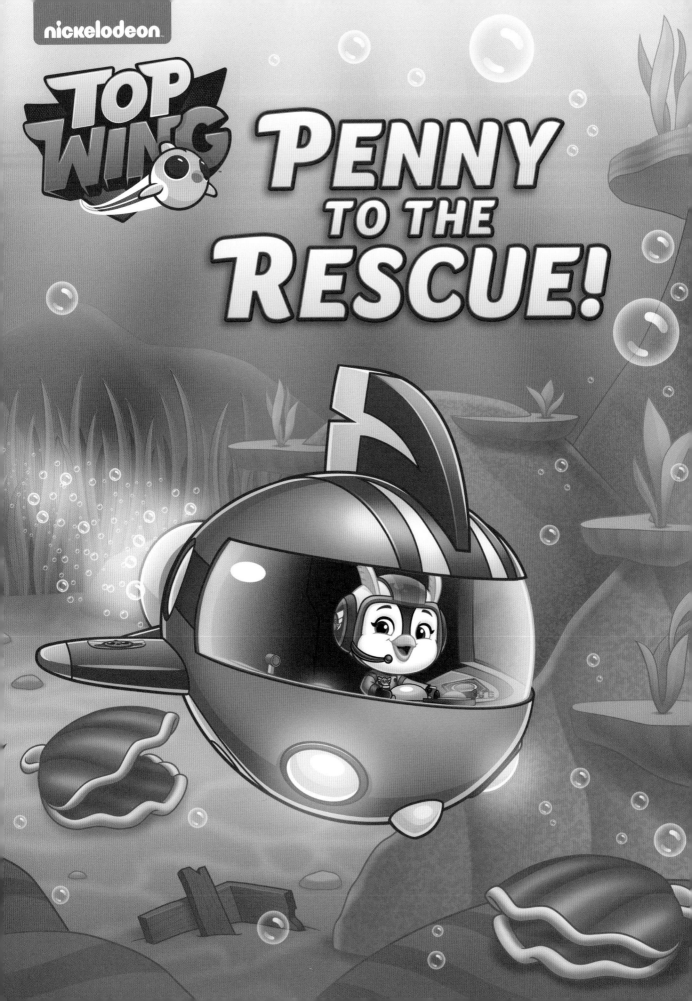

Penny sat in her Aqua Wing while talking to Salty, who was telling her the story of Captain Greenbeard. The captain had hidden a treasure so deep in the ocean, no one could find it.

"Maybe I can find it with my Aqua Wing," Penny said excitedly. She was ready for a treasure hunt!

Unbeknownst to Penny, Cap'n Dilly and Matilda had overheard Salty's story. The pirate crocodiles used their ship's periscope to look for the treasure.

"Let's let Penny find the treasure in her Aqua Wing, and then we'll pirate it from her!" Matilda said.

Back on dry land, Penny told everyone about Captain Greenbeard's hidden treasure.

"It's the most valuable treasure a pirate ever *gobba-gobba* tucked away!" gobbled Commodore Smurkturkski. He put Penny in charge of finding it.

She leapt into her Aqua Wing and took off!

As Penny steered her Aqua Wing underwater, the pirate crocodiles trailed her.

"Right on course, Cap'n!" said Matilda.

"And Penny'll get the treasure for us!" Cap'n Dilly chuckled.

The Aqua Wing's metal detector led Penny toward
a narrow cave in the coral.

She gasped. Something was in the cave!

Penny's sub was too big to fit into the tiny cave, so she hopped onto her mini sub and glided through the entrance.

"There it is!" she shouted. She used the claws on her mini sub to grab the chest. Then she darted back out.

Secretly watching Penny from their ship, the two pirates cheered.

"She found the treasure!" Matilda shouted.

"We're so tricky! We're so clever! We'll make the treasure ours forever! Yo-ho-ho! Arrr!" the pirate crocs sang.

Penny rose out of the water and gave the treasure to the waiting commodore.

"Thank you, Penny!" said Commodore Smurkturkski. "Now let's see the most beautiful treasure in the world!"

But before he could open the chest, Matilda snatched it and swam back toward the pirate ship!

Cap'n Dilly tossed a floating ring to Matilda, and she secured the treasure chest to it. Then Matilda got on the ship, and the two pirate crocodiles sailed off.

"Wait! Come back with my treasure!" shouted Commodore Smurkturkski. He leapt on top of the chest. "Help!"
Penny raced after the pirate ship.

Penny called the other cadets for backup. Brody and Swift caught
up to her, and they all chased Cap'n Dilly and Matilda—straight
into Shipwreck Cove!

"Abandon ship!" shouted Cap'n Dilly.

The pirate crocs jumped into the water.

The cadets flew into action! Swift used the turbo jets on his Flash Wing to turn the ship and stop it from crashing.

Penny used her Aqua Wing's claw to cut the towrope and grab the treasure chest. Brody rescued the commodore with his Splash Wing.

"Oh, that wasn't part of my plan," Cap'n Dilly said, disappointed.

"You mean *arrr* plan," Matilda replied sadly.

On shore, the cadets and their friends gathered around the treasure chest.

"Penny was in charge of saving the treasure . . . but she ended up *gobba-gobba* saving *me*!" cheered Commodore Smurkturkski.

"I just did what any cadet would do," said Penny, smiling.

Commodore Smurkturkski opened the treasure chest to find . . . a little golden pirate ship! It was the best sunken treasure ever.

One sunny afternoon, Princess Nella and Princess Norma were enjoying a tea party in the garden behind the castle. Nella did a trick with a cookie. She used a spoon to catapult it into the air, then caught it on the back of one hand and rolled it up her arm, across her shoulders, and down her other arm. It made Norma giggle with delight!

Hearing the laughter, Trinket trotted over to the sisters. "We're having a best-sisters playdate!" Nella told her. "Care for a spot of lemonade?"

But before Nella could serve Trinket, a giant snowball flew out of the sky and landed on her best unicorn friend!

"How can it be snowing?"
Trinket asked. "There's not a cloud
in the sky!"

"Come on, Norma," said Nella.
"We've got to get you inside."
She picked up her little sister and
carried her into the house.

Just then, Sir Garrett and Clod rushed over.

"Nella! Trinket!" said Sir Garrett. "Giant snowballs are flying all over the kingdom!"

Suddenly, a strange voice echoed from far away. "I'll show you!" it said.

Nella and her friends looked at the two mountains in the distance. They saw a huge creature on top of each peak. Rock Giants!

"They're making a big mess!" said Nella. "And I've got to do something about it. My heart is shining bright—time to be a Princess Knight!"

Nella transformed into a Princess Knight. She and Trinket rode to one peak while Sir Garrett and Clod galloped to the other.

On one snowy mountain, Nella met a Rock Giant named Trevor. Nella learned that Trevor was throwing snow at his little brother, Grud, who was on the other mountain.

"He's such a pain," Trevor grumbled.

Nella had an idea to help the brothers get along. "If you're tired of throwing snowballs at your brother, you could always come to the castle for a tea party. With lots of pretty cups, and lemonade, and cookies . . ."

"Cookies are my favorite! I'd love to come," Trevor said.

Nella transformed her sword into a bow and shot a ribbon arrow with an invitation on it. The arrow sailed all the way to the other peak, where Sir Garrett caught it.

Sir Garrett handed the invitation to Grud.
The giant read the note. "I'm invited to a tea party—
with cookies! I love cookies! Thanks, you guys!"

Later, Nella was preparing for the tea party. Sir Garrett and Clod arrived first with their guest from the mountain.

Grud tried to sit on a chair, but he crushed it with his massive weight.

"Don't worry about that," Nella said, handing him a teacup. Then everyone heard booming footsteps.

It was Trevor!

The two brothers glared at each other and said, "What's *he* doing here?"

The giants scooped up snowballs, ready to fight.

Nella stood between them. "Let's all stay calm and play nice," she said.

But they didn't listen. Trevor threw the first snowball.

"Dragon burps!" Sir Garrett exclaimed when a giant snowball rolled into him.

"Stop throwing snowballs at me, Trevor!" warned Grud.

"No, *you* stop throwing snowballs at *me*, Grud!" Trevor replied.

"Guys!" shouted Nella. "You're brothers! You've got to start getting along."

Nella thought of what both brothers loved—cookies! She quickly showed everyone her trick.

"Too bad we don't have a giant spoon," said Trevor, "so we could do what you were doing."

Nella smiled. "Maybe this will do."

She transformed her sword into a lance and handed it to Trevor. He balanced it on a rock and put a cookie on one end.

"Here you go, little bro," Trevor said as he swatted the handle of the lance. The cookie popped into the air.

Grud caught the cookie, ate it in one bite, and yelled, "Again!"

Nella looked around happily. "Now, *this* is a tea party."

Trevor smiled at his little brother. "You know, you can be kind of fun, little bro."

Grud smiled back at his big brother. "You too, big bro."

Norma looked up at her big sister and cooed.

"I really couldn't agree more, Norma," said Nella as she reached down and hugged her little sister.

The best sisters—and the best brothers—enjoyed the rest of the tea party with their friends!

Princess Samira had exciting news for Shimmer, Shine, and Leah. They were going to travel to Zahramay Skies and learn about Stardust Magic from Adara, the Stardust Princess!

She gave each girl a special ring. When they pressed the center and said, *"Zahraflash!"* three beautiful winged Zahracorns appeared!

The girls flew on their new Zahracorn friends. "This is so fun!" Shimmer cried.

Zeta and her pet dragon, Nazboo, watched from a distance. She wanted to know where they were going. But first she needed more magic-carpet dust for her scooter!

The girls soon arrived in Zahramay Skies.
"Hello!" said a friendly voice. "I'm Adara, the Stardust Princess. Welcome!"
The girls were excited to meet Princess Adara.

Zahramay Skies was an incredible place. Wherever the genies looked, they saw beautiful clouds, pretty trees, and star-tastic rainbows.

They couldn't wait to learn Stardust Magic!

Inside Princess Adara's palace, Leah began to float!

"Leah's not a genie! How is that even *possible*?" Shine asked.

"Oh, everyone floats in Zahramay Skies," Princess Adara explained.

Once they had all settled in, they were ready to learn about Stardust Magic.

"I'll start by teaching you about the different kinds of stars," Princess Adara said. She showed them shooting stars, shining stars, rainbow stars, dreaming stars, musical stars, surprise stars, and wishing stars.

Princess Adara gave the girls their own star wands.

Shimmer's wand made everything extra shiny.

Leah's wand made beautiful rainbows.

Shine's wand would grant the holder one wish!

Meanwhile, Zeta had gotten a bottle of powerful stardust, which transformed her scooter into a glider!

Zeta flew to Zahramay Skies. She found the genies—and the stars!

"I want them all!" she cried. "Then I'll be the most powerful person in Genie World!"

With a disappearing potion, she made the palace dome vanish so the stars would float out into the sky.

"The stars!" Shimmer exclaimed when she saw them moving toward Zeta.

"You girls need to stop that sorceress!" Princess Adara told them.

They were ready for action. They climbed onto their Zahracorns and headed for Zeta.

Zeta wished that all the stars would come to her, and Shine's wishing-star wand granted her wish.

"Now all the stardust will be mine!" she said.

But the stars zoomed straight at Zeta and Nazboo! The sorceress and her pet tried to hide, and the stars kept after them.

The girls followed the stars straight to Zeta.
"Do something!" Zeta shrieked.
"Maybe if our Zahracorns flap their wings hard enough, they can keep the stars away!" Shine suggested.

Her plan worked!
"Way to go, Zahracorns!" Shimmer said.

Just then, Princess Adara arrived. "Looks like you could use some help!" she said. "Allow me." Using her powers, she released the stars from Zeta's magic.

"She did it!" Shine cheered.

"Now who wants to help me return the stars to my palace?" Adara asked.

"I do!" Shimmer, Shine, and Leah said.

"Ugh," Zeta grumbled. "Fine."

"Nazboo help, too!" the little dragon exclaimed.

Soon all the stars were safely back where they belonged. Everyone celebrated with yummy Staracones!

Butterbean was flying through the town of Puddlebrook. Her two best friends, Poppy and Dazzle, and her little sister, Cricket, tried to keep up.

"What are you so excited about, Butterbean?" asked Dazzle.

"You'll see," Butterbean promised.

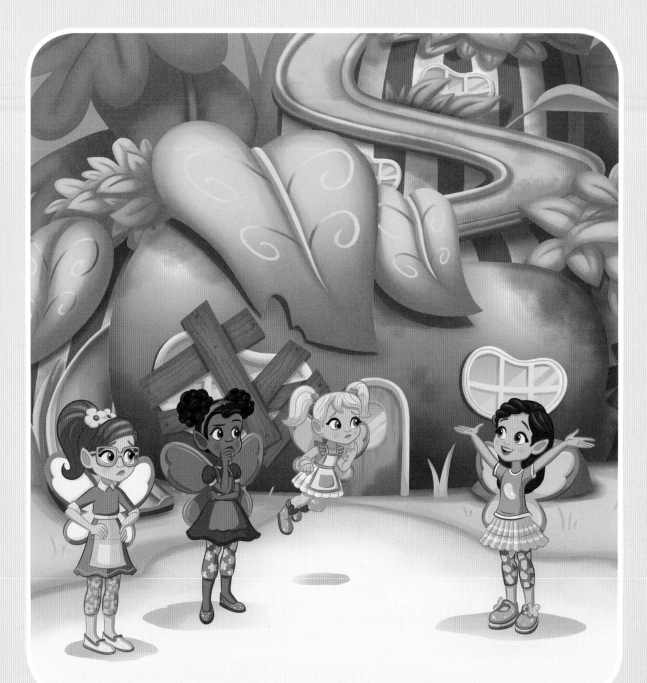

Finally, Butterbean landed near an old building.

"*Ta-da!*" she announced. "This is our new café!"

"It doesn't *look* very new," Poppy said skeptically, eyeing the boarded-up building.

"It will be when we fix it up," Butterbean replied.

Butterbean had great plans. Poppy would run the kitchen, Dazzle would take care of the front counter, and Cricket would help everyone. "With a pinch of patience and a helping of hard work, I know we can make this the fairy best café in all of Puddlebrook!" Butterbean declared to her friends.

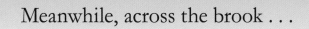
Meanwhile, across the brook . . .

. . . there was another café—Marmalady's Café! It was run by Ms. Marmalady and her assistants, Spork and Spatch.

Ms. Marmalady served only one thing—marma-loaf! It was green, gloppy, smelly, and not very appetizing. But hers was the only café in town, and that was just the way she liked it. Ms. Marmalady didn't know that the fairy friends were getting Butterbean's Café ready for its grand opening. . . .

One day while working in the old building, Cricket discovered a mysterious box. She showed it to her sister. Butterbean noticed FOR THE FAIRY FINISH written on it. When she read the words aloud, sparkles began to dance around the box. The top opened and a magical whisk floated out!

Butterbean waved the whisk, and a trail of sparkles made the girls' wings look like yummy sugar cookies! The whisk also exchanged Poppy's spoon for a magical one, gave Dazzle a magical stylus, and made Cricket a special icing bag.

The girls used their new magical tools to put the finishing touches on the café.

Just then, the front door opened and a boy on a skateboard zipped in.

"My name's Jasper," said the boy. "Wow, you really fixed up this old place."

Butterbean thanked him and explained that it was the café's opening day. She told him that most of their ingredients would be ordered fresh from nearby farms, and she could use a speedy delivery person like him.

Butterbean offered Jasper a job at the café. And with her magical whisk, she even gave him really fast wings.

"I'm the newest member of the Bean Team!" he said proudly. Then he and Cricket flew off to deliver the invitations for the café's grand opening.

At her own café, Ms. Marmalady was spying on her new neighbors. "Do they think they can just fly into town and open a brand-new café?" she muttered.

She didn't want anyone to go to Butterbean's grand opening, so she ordered Spork and Spatch to steal all the invitations Cricket and Jasper delivered.

Meanwhile, Butterbean was busy baking wing-shaped cookies when she noticed some writing on her whisk. It was a spell! She read it aloud: *"'With a flick of this whisk and a flutter of wing, these magical beans will do their thing.'"*

Suddenly, colorful beans magically filled the box. There was a Sparkle Bean, a Swirly Bean, and even a Flutter Bean.

A magical whisk and magical beans? Butterbean was thrilled! There really *was* something special about her café!

Soon the girls were ready to open the café and greet their customers!

But when they looked out the front door, no one was there.

"There's got to be something we can do," Butterbean said, determined to save the grand opening.

That was when she remembered the magical beans. She chose one, then waved her whisk over it and said the spell, with a few minor changes: *"With a flick of this whisk and a flutter of wing, the Flutter Bean will do its thing."*

The wing-shaped cookies flew off the counter and fluttered through Puddlebrook, leading a crowd of townspeople to the café. Even Spork and Spatch were unable to resist the magic.

"Oh, freezer burn," Ms. Marmalady grumbled. She knew Butterbean's Café was going to be a huge success.

Butterbean's Café was officially open for business!

Everest and Jake were enjoying a cold day whale watching. "Whoa!" Jake cried. "Up ahead! I see something moving in the water."

He was pointing to a whale! The whale gave a loud, sad cry. Jake and Everest thought the whale was looking for something.

Using his binoculars,
Jake looked left and right.
He spotted a baby whale in
the distance! But it looked
trapped in the ice.

Everest and Jake steered the boat to the ice and climbed down. They slipped and slid their way toward the baby whale.

"I bet it's trying to find its mom," Jake said when they reached it.

But it was too far away from the open water. Jake knew just what to do—call the PAW Patrol!

Ryder answered Jake's call, and Jake and Everest quickly explained the problem.

"We're on our way!" Ryder responded. "No job is too big, no pup is too small. PAW Patrol, to the Air Patroller!"

The pups ran toward the vehicle, ready to help their friends. Robo Dog flew them north after picking up Rubble's construction rig. During the flight, Ryder explained the plan. It would be a major team effort!

The pups landed and got right to work.
First, Rubble used his rig to drill air holes in the ice
so the baby whale could breathe.

Then Rocky used his saw to make the holes big enough for the whale to fit through.

Finally, Everest pulled the ice chunks away with her big hook.

"Ice or snow, I'm ready to go!" Everest said as she ran back to the team.

143

The work was done, but the whale was still under the ice.

"Pups, we've gotta keep leading that baby whale toward the ocean," Ryder said.

The baby whale didn't seem to understand. It just wanted to play with the pups! That gave Ryder an idea.

"Everest, do you think you could get the baby to chase you on your snowboard?" Ryder asked.

"Tag? I'm it!" Everest replied as she hopped onto her board.

"Betcha can't catch me, baby," Everest said to the whale as she took off toward the next air hole.

She jumped . . .

flipped over the hole . . .

and stuck the landing!

"Come on, follow me!"
Everest called to the baby.
With a wiggle, the baby
whale jumped . . .

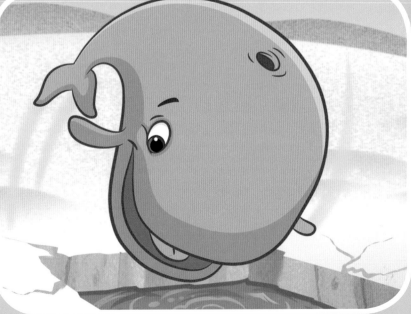

flipped over the ice . . .

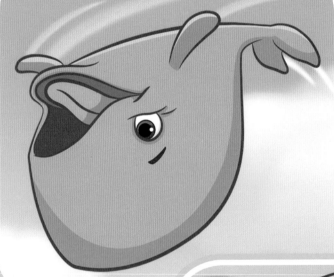

and dove into
the water!

Everest and the baby whale went back and forth until, with one last, giant jump, the baby whale dived into the ocean.

The baby whale happily swam to its mommy. The mommy whale nuzzled her baby, then gave a cry of thanks to the pups.